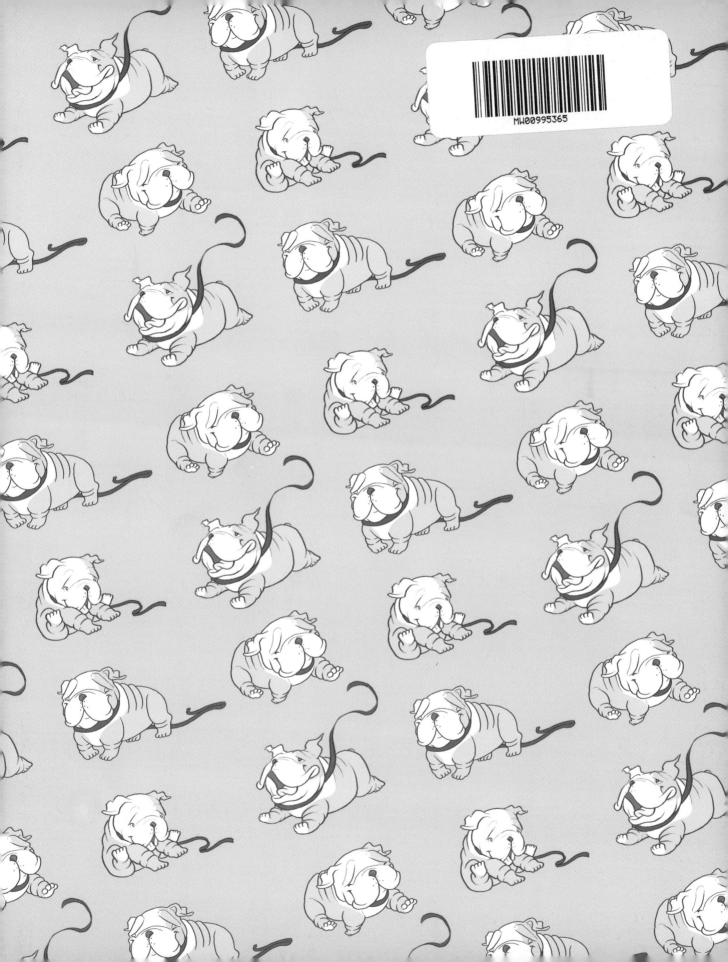

Good Boy, Blue!

Requests for permission to make copies of any part of the work should be submitted online at info@mascotbooks.com or mailed to Mascot Books, 560 Herndon Parkway #120, Herndon, VA 20170.

The indicia featured in this book are registered trademarks of Butler University.

PRT0614B

Printed in the United States

ISBN-13: 9781937406806
ISBN-10: 1937406806

www.mascotbooks.com

GOOD BOY, BLUE!

Written by
MICHAEL KALTENMARK

Illustrated by
JINGO M. DE LA ROSA

For Butler Blue II.
-MK

At just seven weeks old, a dog named Blue left the farm for Butler University.

His Pops said, "It's time to be a good boy, Blue!"

Blue wasn't sure he knew what it meant to be a "good boy,"
but he liked the way those words sounded.
He wanted to hear them again and again.

Blue and Pops arrived at Butler.

Students and teachers "oooed," "aaahd," whistled, and cheered at the sight of their new mascot.

Walking just as fast as his little bulldog legs would carry him, Blue beamed with pride.

He felt great, but not as great as when he heard the words, "Good boy, Blue."

Pops stopped in front of the great Jordan Hall.

He told Blue, "This is where professors teach and students learn."

Inside, Pops tugged Blue into the office of the university president.

Blue could sense he was a man in charge.

"How about a treat?" the president asked as he reached into his desk drawer.
Blue's ears went up and back. He knew the word, "treat."

The president held the treat above Blue's head. Blue knew what to do.
He quickly sat and stared patiently, drooling just a bit.

Impressed, the president chuckled as he gave Blue the treat.
He said, "What nice manners you have. Good boy, Blue."

Blue loved those words even more than the treat he was chomping.

Blue trotted with Pops for what seemed like forever.

Finally, they arrived at historic Hinkle Fieldhouse.

To Blue, it looked like one big, red brick dog house.

With a whistle around his neck, the Bulldogs' basketball coach
stood on the court watching the players practice their famous team defense.

Without warning, Blue took a flying leap at Coach's basketball.

WOOOSH!

THUD!

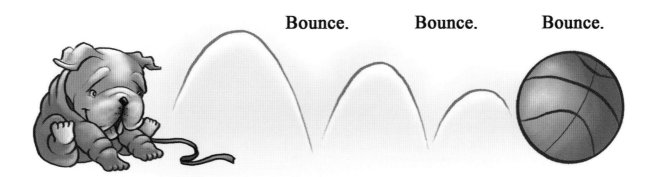

Bounce.   Bounce.   Bounce.

Heavy panting echoed off the Fieldhouse walls.

After a moment of quiet, the rafters filled with the sound of the team's laughter.

Pops quickly grabbed Blue and apologized to Coach.

"So this is our new mascot, eh?" Coach asked.

"Yes, sir," replied Pops.

"You've got a nose for the ball," Coach told Blue.

"You'll sure fit in well around here. Good boy, Blue."

Those words again!

Blue stood tall on his new basketball court.

Pops led Blue toward the Irwin Library.
The librarian wanted to meet
Butler's famous new mascot.

The library was a quiet place.

Students studied in every nook and cranny.
Some read books. Others took notes.

Blue did his best to be quiet, too.

Suddenly, a book fell from a high shelf
and came crashing down on the floor.

SMACK!

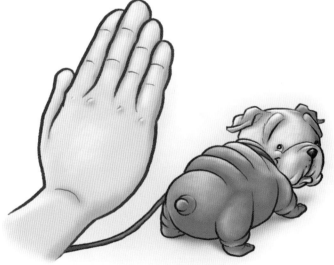

Normally, Blue would have barked
with surprise, but Pops held out
his palm as if to say STOP!

Blue quickly closed his mouth.

He held the bark in, like a sneeze.

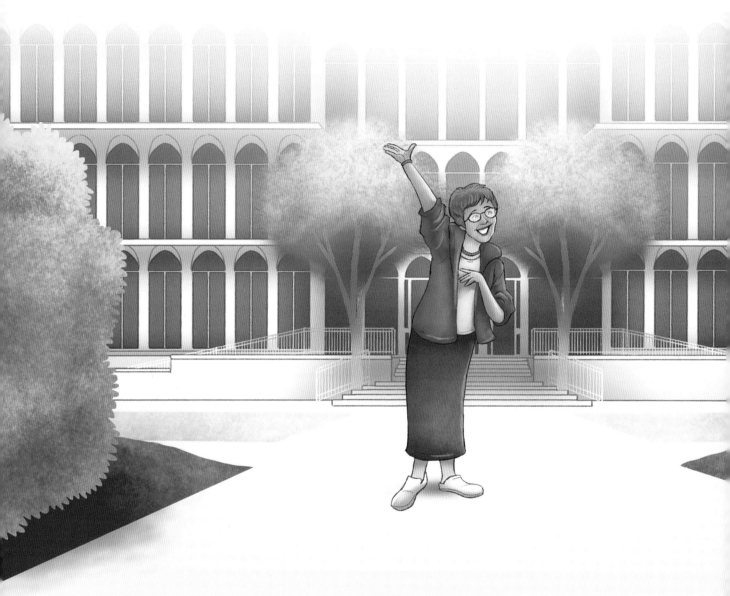

The librarian smiled. Pleased with Blue, she said,
"Our mascot is welcome in the library any time. Good boy, Blue."

Blue knew that holding in that bark was worth it.

Blue and Pops left the library and made their way to the Atherton Student Union.

On the way, they came across a professor and her sweet
St. Bernard named Freckles.

Freckles excitedly wagged his tail at Blue,
but Blue crouched low, showed his teeth, and snarled.

This was his campus, he wanted to say.

At the sound of a growl, Pops pulled Blue's leash
and sternly said, "Bad dog! Bad boy, Blue!"

Blue's heart sank. He knew he had done wrong.

Blue felt sorry. He disappointed Pops, hurt Freckles' feelings,
and missed an opportunity to hear his favorite words.

Just outside the union, hundreds of people gathered to welcome Blue to campus.

Blue saw lots of Butler fans, including his new pals the University president, Coach, and the librarian.

Even Freckles was there.

Everybody clapped and cheered and smiled at Blue.
But Blue wasn't sure that he deserved it.
After all, he let Pops down when he had growled at Freckles.

The president said some words to the crowd.

Then he handed Blue his official mascot jersey and a tasty dog bone.

Blue had an idea.

He took the bone right over to Freckles.
He bit it in half,
and nudged one part over to the sweet dog.

Freckles beamed.

Butler's famous mascot
was sharing his special treat with him!

Pops leaned down and whispered into Blue's floppy ear.
He told Blue that he was proud of him for being a good sharer.

Then he said those words:

"You're a good boy, Blue!"

Coach patted Blue on the head and said, "Atta boy, Blue!"

Very soon, everybody was saying,

"Good boy, Blue. Good boy!"

THE END

 # BUTLER UNIVERSITY

Home of the Bulldogs, Butler University is a
private, liberal arts institution located on nearly
300 beautiful acres in Indianapolis, Indiana.
The University offers more than 60 majors across
six colleges, 19 NCAA Division 1 teams,
and one beautiful English Bulldog mascot named
Butler Blue, who enjoys eating ice cream and
posing for pictures with campus visitors.

Learn more about Butler at butler.edu
and more about Blue at ButlerBlue.com.

Go Dawgs!

ABOUT THE AUTHOR

MICHAEL KALTENMARK

is both a Butler University graduate and staff member, but he is probably best known as the caretaker for the school's live English Bulldog mascots, Butler Blue II and Butler Blue III. He lives in Indianapolis, Indiana with his family of dog lovers—his wife and son —and enjoys competing in triathlons and listening to music.

ABOUT THE ILLUSTRATOR

JINGO M. DE LA ROSA

is an illustrator and character artist whose love affair with drawing dates back to his childhood. Born and raised in the Philippines, he now lives in Bloomington, Indiana with his wife, a Butler University graduate.

Learn more about Jingo and his illustrations at www.jingoillo.com.

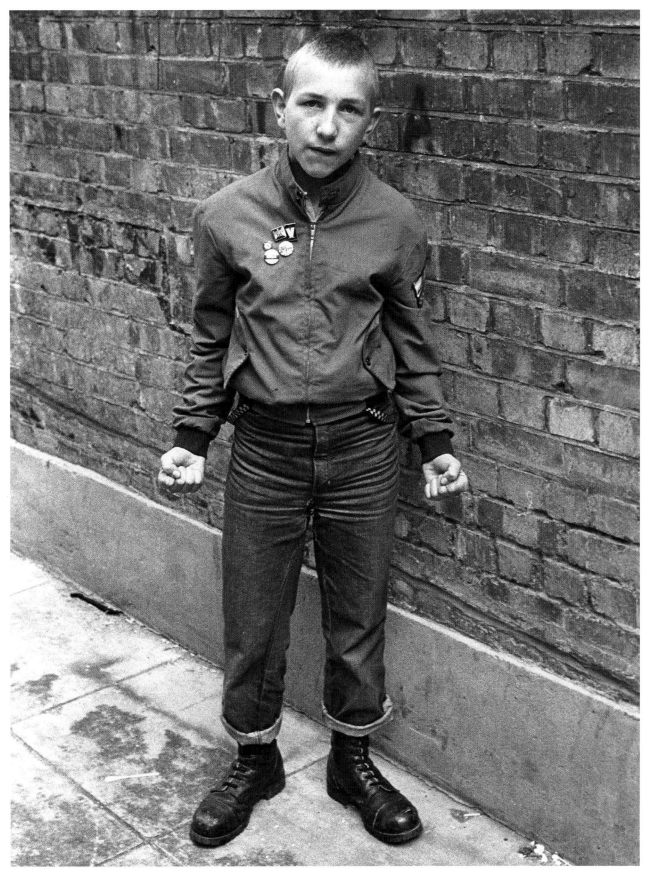

This spread: Dirk, Feltham, 1980

Hastings, 1981

This spread: Wayne aka Smiler, near Carnaby Street, 1984

Mark, Shoreditch, 1980

Rob, Shoreditch, 1980

Near Carnaby Street, 1981

Hanway Street, 1982

Chelsea, 1981

Chelsea, 1981

Near Carnaby Street, 1984

Outside the Blade Bone, Hoxton, 1979

Shoreditch, 1979

94

Shoreditch, 1979

This spread: Outside The Last Resort in Goulston Street, Aldgate, 1981

Carrie, outside The Last Resort in Goulston Street, Aldgate, 1981

Kevin, outside The Last Resort in Goulston Street, Aldgate, 1981

Outside The Last Resort in Goulston Street, Aldgate, 1981

Donna, Leicester Square, 1982

Outside The Last Resort in Goulston Street, Aldgate, 1981

Kensal Rise, 1983

This spread: Mark, Leicester Square, 1981

This spread: Nicky Crane, Shoreditch, 1979

Nicky and Tracey after their wedding, Welling, 1980

This spread: House party in Stoke Newington, 1981

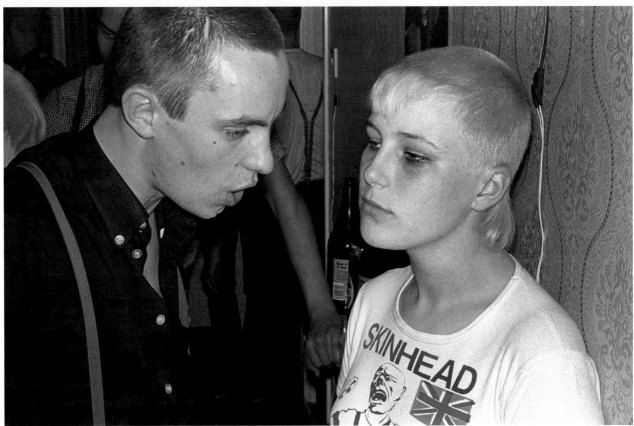

This page: House party in Stoke Newington, 1981

Leicester Square, 1981

Hammersmith tube station, 1981

This page: On the tube, West London, 1981

Near Carnaby Street, 1984

Chelsea, 1980

Hastings, 1981

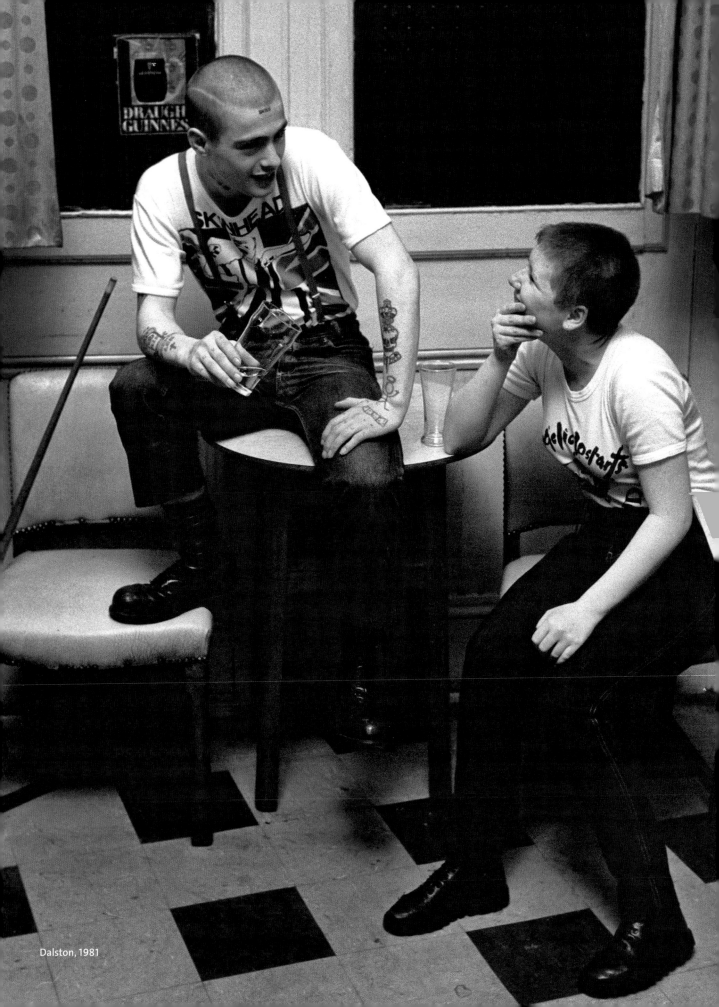

Dalston, 1981

This page: Southwark, 1981

123

This spread: Outside the Crown and Shuttle, Shoreditch, 1979

Tuinol Barry, near Carnaby Street, 1980

Brighton, 1980

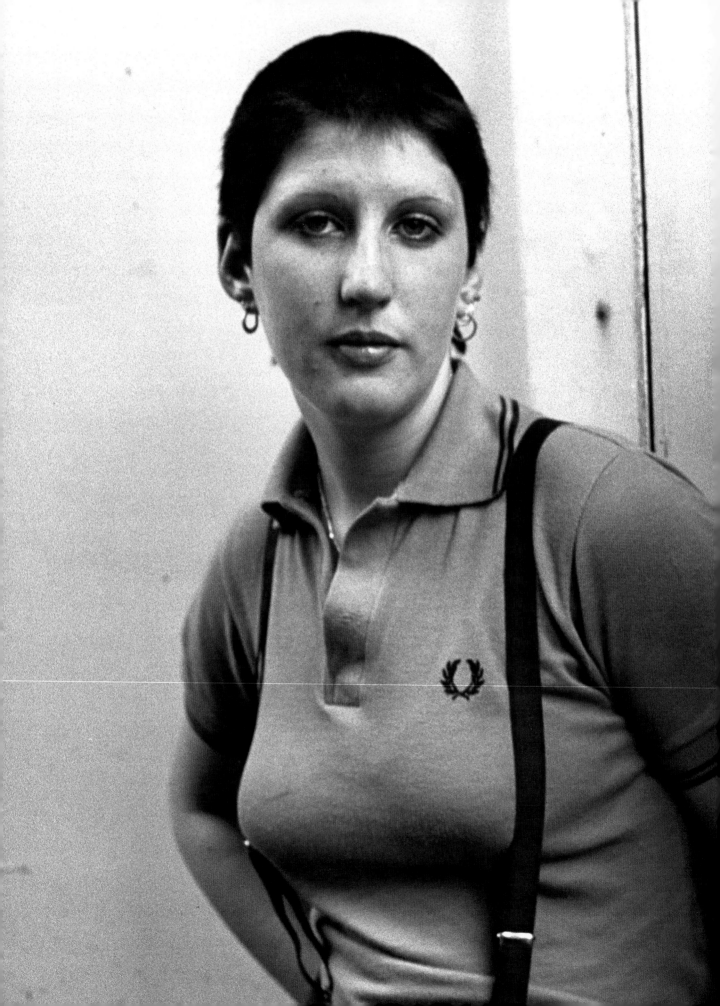

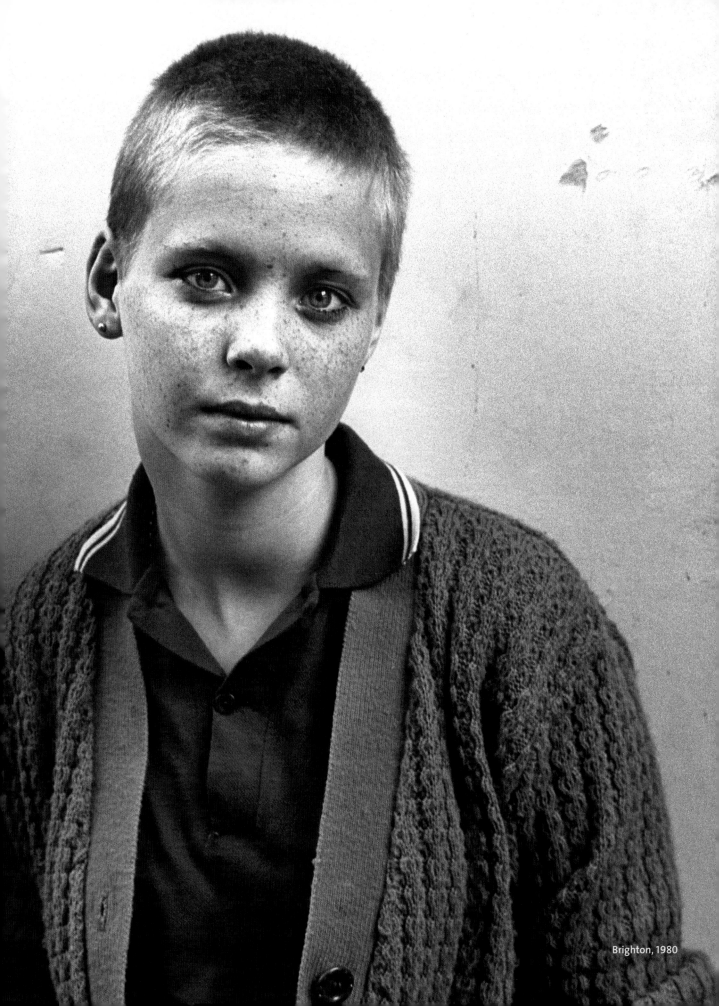

Brighton, 1980

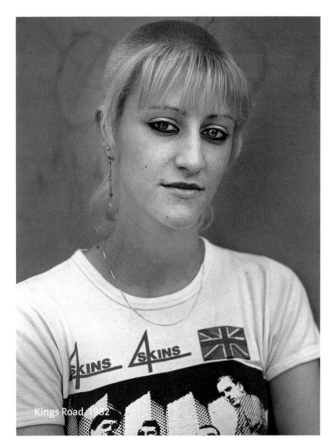

Kings Road, 1982

Brockwell Park, 1983

Brixton, 1981

Kings Road, 1982

130

Margate, 1982

Chelsea, 1981

Hastings, 1981

Chelsea, 1981

Margate, 1980

Chelsea, 1982

Aldgate, 1979

135

NOW SHOWING
2 HOUR SHOW

Leicester Square, 1981

Chelsea, 1981

Kate and Lesley, Shoreditch, 1979

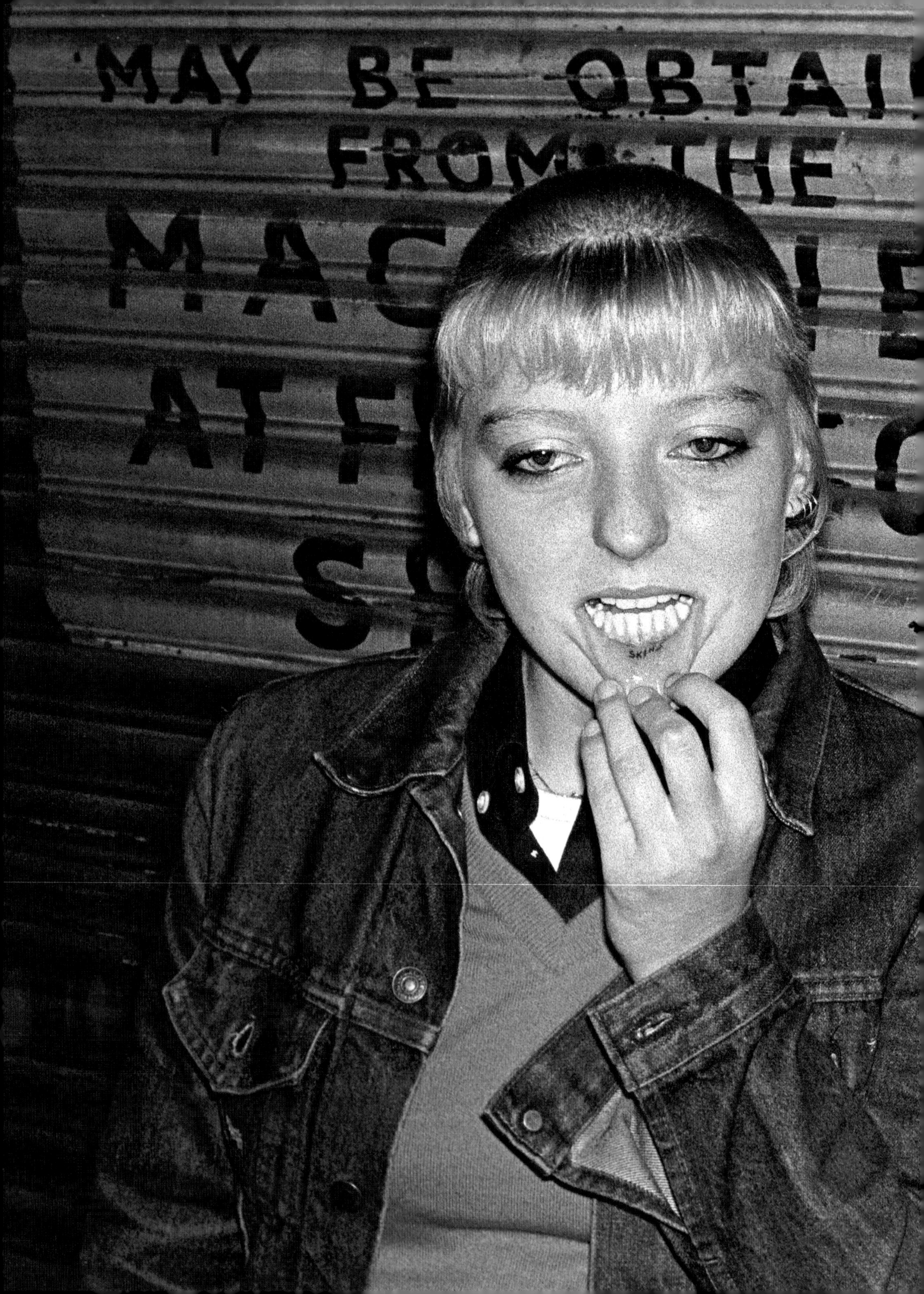
MAY BE OBTAI
FROM THE

Dawn and Becky, Putney Station, 1980

Tattoo parlour in Walworth Road, Southwark, 1982

Near Carnaby Street, 1982

144

Kings Road, Chelsea, 1981

145

Carrie, Aldgate, 1981

Rob, Shoreditch, 1979

147

Johnny, Leicester Square, 1980

This spread: Chris, Hanway Street, 1982

John and Dave, Chelsea, 1981

Chelsea, 1981

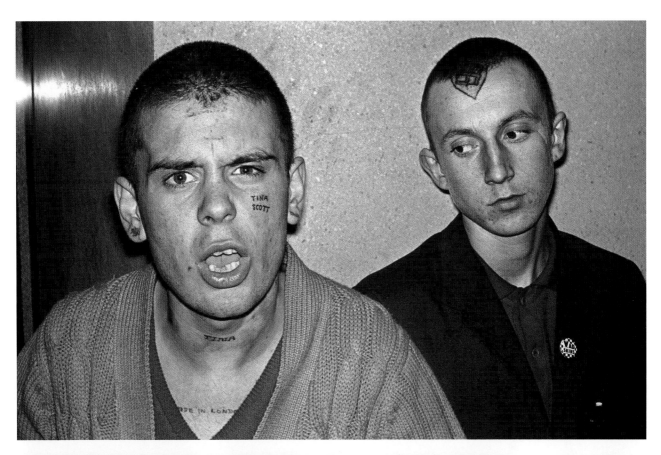

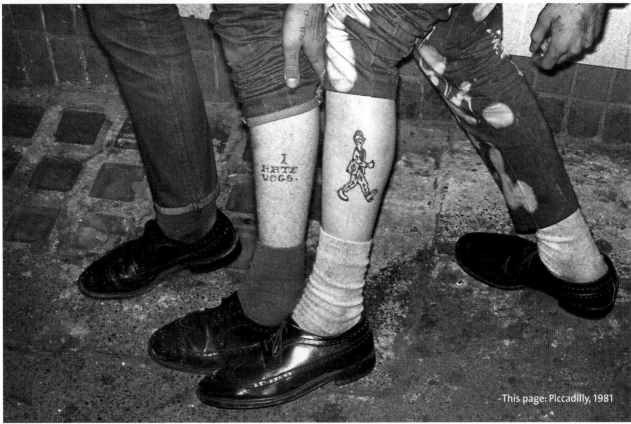

This page: Piccadilly, 1981

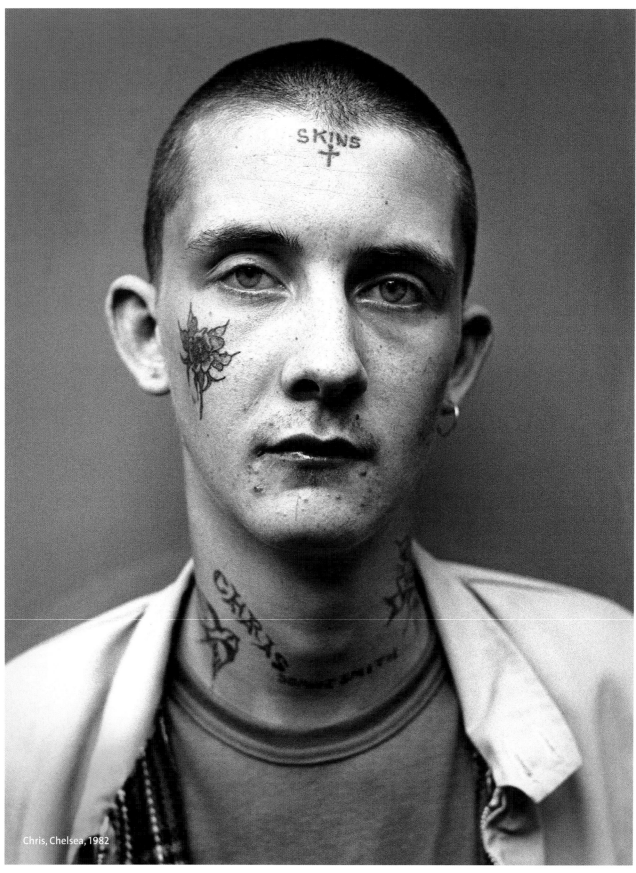

Chris, Chelsea, 1982

Soho, 1984

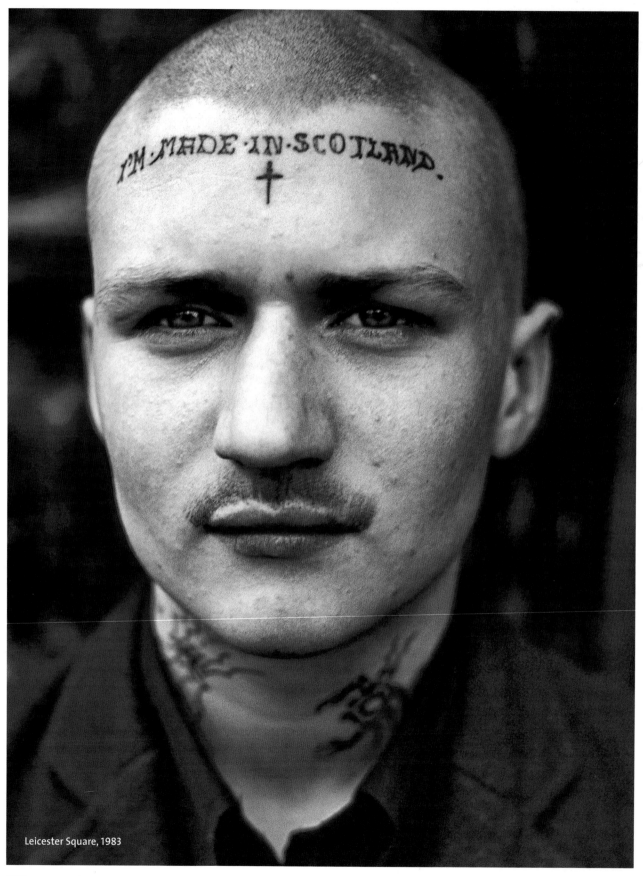

Leicester Square, 1983

Tuinol Barry, Chelsea, 1981

Chelsea, 1981